Disney

Snow White
and the Seven Dwarfs

KU-351-657

AUTUMN
PUBLISHING

Long ago, there lived a kind princess named Snow White.
Her wicked stepmother, the Queen, feared that some day
Snow White's beauty would outshine her own, so she forced
the princess to dress in rags and work like a servant.
But nothing could spoil Snow White's sweet nature.

Each day, the Queen consulted her Magic Mirror. She always asked the same question: "Magic Mirror, on the wall, who is the fairest one of all?"

And each day the Mirror replied, "You are the fairest one of all."

But one morning, the Mirror said that Snow White was the most beautiful woman in all the land! The Queen flew into a jealous rage.

Meanwhile, Snow White attended to her chores and sang a wish into a wishing well. She hoped that, some day soon, she would meet a prince and fall in love. Little did she know that a handsome prince had overheard her song!

The Prince fell in love with the princess instantly. Snow White was shy at first and fled back to the castle, but as the Prince sang a love song, she began to fall in love, too.

The next morning, the jealous Queen plotted against the princess. She ordered her royal huntsman to take Snow White far into the forest, kill her and bring back her heart in a box.

The huntsman led the princess into the forest but he could not bring himself to kill her. He told Snow White to hide and he took an animal's heart back to the Queen instead.

Snow White wandered deep into the forest. She was scared, but some friendly woodland animals led her to a little cottage.

"Oh, it's adorable!" Snow White cried. "Just like a doll's house." She tried the door and it swung open.

"Hello? May I come in?" Snow White called, but no one answered.

Snow White stepped inside the cottage and saw seven little chairs. She thought that seven little children must live there.

"And from the look of this table, seven untidy little children!" she said, then held up a rather smelly sock.

"We'll clean the house and surprise them!" said Snow White. "Then maybe they'll let me stay."

So, with the help of her forest friends, Snow White dusted and cleaned the little cottage. Then she lay across three of the tiny beds and fell fast asleep.

Evening came and the owners of the cottage made their way home. They were seven dwarfs, who worked in diamond mines deep in the heart of a mountain.

Singing a jolly tune as they marched along, they had no idea of the surprise waiting for them!

As soon as they entered the cottage, they knew something wasn't quite right. Their home had been cleaned! The floor had been swept and there was a delicious smell coming from a pot on the fire.

"There's dirty work afoot!" grumbled the dwarf called Grumpy.

The Seven Dwarfs searched the cottage for an intruder. They reached the bedroom just as Snow White was waking up.

They hid at the end of their beds and gazed at her curiously.

"How do you do!" said Snow White. She then guessed each of their names from the etchings on the end of their beds. They were called Doc, Bashful, Sleepy, Sneezy, Happy, Dopey, and Grumpy.

"I'm Snow White," she said, and she told them all about the evil Queen and why she had fled into the forest. "Please don't send me away," she pleaded.

The Dwarfs felt sorry for Snow White and agreed to let her stay.

That evening, the cottage was filled with music and laughter.
After enjoying a delicious dinner cooked by Snow White, the
Dwarfs sang and danced to welcome the princess to their home.

Snow White was so happy that she soon forgot all about her
wicked stepmother.

Meanwhile, back in the castle, the Queen was standing in front of her Magic Mirror. She asked the question she always asked, but instead of answering as she expected, the Mirror replied:

"Snow White still lives, the fairest in the land. It's the heart of a pig you hold in your hand."

The Queen gasped in horror – the huntsman had tricked her!

The Queen stormed down a winding staircase and through a dark dungeon to a hidden room in the castle. There, she found her book of magic spells and used a terrible potion to transform herself into an old woman!

Next, she dipped an apple into a bubbling cauldron.

"One taste of the poisoned apple and the victim's eyes will close forever!" she said.

The only antidote to the Queen's spell was Love's First Kiss.

The next day, after the Dwarfs had left for work, Snow White was visited by the disguised Queen.

The birds and forest animals watched in alarm as kind-hearted Snow White took the old woman inside the cottage for a cup of water. They knew the princess was in terrible danger, so they raced to the mines to fetch the Seven Dwarfs.

The Queen offered Snow White the poisoned apple.

"It's a magic wishing apple," she lied. "Now take the apple, dearie, and make a wish."

Snow White took the apple and thought of the handsome prince. "I wish... I wish..." she whispered.

Snow White closed her eyes and took a single bite. A moment later, she fell to the floor.

"Now I'll be the fairest in the land!" the Queen cackled.

As the Queen left the cottage, the Dwarfs arrived and chased after her. They followed her through the forest and up a mountain. Higher and higher the Queen went until she came to a stop at the edge of a cliff. There was nowhere else to go.

CRACK! A bolt of lightning struck the ledge where the evil Queen stood. The ledge crumbled and with a shriek the Queen fell, never to be seen again.

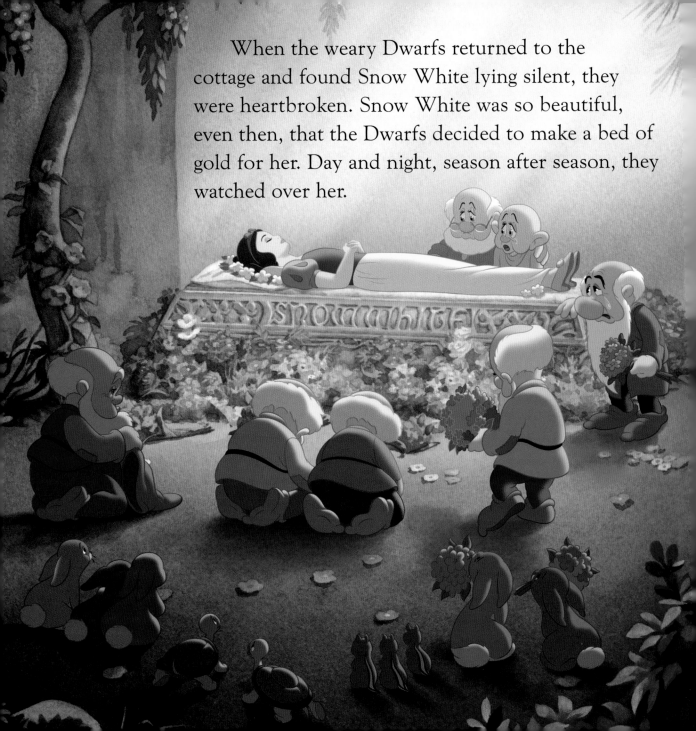

When the weary Dwarfs returned to the cottage and found Snow White lying silent, they were heartbroken. Snow White was so beautiful, even then, that the Dwarfs decided to make a bed of gold for her. Day and night, season after season, they watched over her.

Then, one afternoon, a handsome young man came riding through the forest. He was the Prince who had fallen in love with Snow White by the castle well.

The handsome Prince had searched far and wide for the princess he had met that fateful morning. When he came to the clearing where Snow White lay, he leaned over and kissed her. It was Love's First Kiss!

With a soft sigh,
Snow White sat up
and rubbed her eyes.
The Prince shouted
with joy and lifted her
up in his arms.

The Dwarfs
danced and laughed,
and the woods rang
with calls from the
happy forest animals.
Snow White was
awake!

Before she left to begin her new life with the Prince, Snow White kissed each of the Seven Dwarfs goodbye and promised to visit them soon.

Lifting her onto his horse, the Prince led Snow White to his castle, where they would live happily ever after.